HOW SPIDER SAVED THANKSGIVING

BY ROBERT KRAUS

SCHOLASTIC INC.

New York Toronto London Auckland Sydney

ISBN 0-590-44411-5

Copyright © 1991 by Robert Kraus.
All rights reserved. Published by Scholastic Inc.

12 11 10 9 8 7 6 5 4 3 2 1   1 2 3 4 5 6/9

Printed in the U.S.A.   24

First Scholastic printing, October 1991

Thanksgiving was coming, and I was feeling happy.

"What's your favorite holiday, Fly?" I asked.
"Halloween," said Fly. "I like to scare other bugs."
"I love all holidays," said Ladybug.

Then the school bell rang. Brrrrrrrinnnnnggggg!
We all hurried into Miss Quito's class.

"Good-morning, class," said Miss Quito.
"Today I'm going to tell you about the very first Thanksgiving."

"Zzzzzzzzzz," snored the twin caterpillars.
They just couldn't stay awake.

"The Pilgrims came over on the *Mayflower*," said Miss Quito.

"That fly is my uncle Max," said Fly.
"Shhh," said Ladybug.

"And here is a picture of the Pilgrims celebrating the first Thanksgiving with their neighbors, the Indians," said Miss Quito. "I'm a *Mayflower* fly," said Fly.

"We are going to put on a play about the first Thanksgiving," said Miss Quito.
"I'll be a Pilgrim," said Fly.
"I'll be a Pilgrim lady," said Ladybug.
"Very good," said Miss Quito. "Everyone else can be Indians!"

We rehearsed the play every day.

Finally the day of the show arrived.
The first act was on the good ship *Mayflower*.
"Sail on," said Fly.
"Water, water everywhere," said Ladybug, "and not
a drop to drink."

"Have a drink from my canteen," I said.

I was also playing a Pilgrim as we were short of bugs. "Land ho!" shouted Fly as the curtain fell.

I changed into an Indian for the next act, and
greeted Fly and Ladybug as they landed
on Plymouth Rock.
"Welcome, Pilgrims," I said.

"We come in peace," said Fly.
"I think Pilgrim Fly speaks with
forked tongue," I said.

The curtain dropped.
Miss Quito applauded.

Act three was the Thanksgiving feast.
We were all seated around the Thanksgiving table.
The table was set, but there was no turkey.

"Oh, my," said Miss Quito. "I forgot to bring the turkey!"
And what was Thanksgiving without a turkey?

Everybody looked at me.
"Don't look at *me*," I said.
Then I got an idea!

I rushed into the supply closet
and found what I was looking for —
a box of balloons!

I huffed and puffed and blew up ten balloons.
Then I twisted and turned, and turned and twisted,
until...

There was our turkey!

"You've saved the play,
Spider!" said Ladybug.

The balloon turkey was the hit of the show.
The audience applauded.
But we were still hungry.

So after the show we went to Ladybug's house and had a *real* Thanksgiving dinner.

And we gave thanks…
Fly for the good food.
Ladybug for good times.
Miss Quito for good students.

And me for my good friends,
Fly and Ladybug
— and a great teacher, Miss Quito.